THE **KNIGHT** OF STICKS AND STRAW

TERRY DEARY'S KNIGHTS' TALES

THE KNIGHT OF STICKS AND STRAW

Illustrated by Helen Flook

A & C Black • London

First published 2009 by
A & C Black
an imprint of Bloomsbury Publishing Plc
50 Bedford Square, London, WC1B 3DP

www.bloomsbury.com

Text copyright © 2009 Terry Deary
Illustrations copyright © 2009 Helen Flook

ISBN 978-1-4081-0621-1

A CIP catalogue for this book is available from the British Library.

This book is produced using paper that is made from wood grown
in managed, sustainable forests. It is natural, renewable and
recyclable. The logging and manufacturing processes conform to the
environmental regulations of the country of origin.

Printed and Bound by CPI Group (UK) Ltd, Croydon CR0 4YY

3 5 7 9 10 8 6 4 2

Chapter One
Bullies
and Berbers

Castile, Spain, 1099

Cristina hated the feasts at the palace of Valencia.

The knights made a lot of noise and shouted at her. But that wasn't why she hated the feasts.

The cooks in the kitchen made her run and fetch heavy bags of corn, pots big enough for her to bathe in and logs that were larger than her. But that wasn't why she hated the feasts.

The maids poked fun at her tattered, woollen clothes and her bare feet, for she only had shoes for church on Sunday. They bullied her. But that wasn't why she hated the feasts.

The feasts went on deep into the night. By the time Cristina had helped clear the tables, clean the pots and polish the pans, it was dark.

Even in the warm, summer nights, when the stars were like a shower of silver, it was dark in the streets of Valencia when she hurried home. *That* was why she hated the feasts.

Everyone was asleep as Cristina ran home over the stony streets, past snarling dogs, slippery rats and green-eyed cats. And worse.

That first night, she almost lost her way from the palace gates to her home on the hill below. She crashed through the door into the poor, little house and the leather hinges almost snapped.

Cristina's mother gasped in the blackness. "Who's there?"

Cristina panted for breath and creaked like the door. "Mama!"

"Cristina? Are you back?"

"Mama!"

"What on earth is wrong, child?"

"I saw a giant... He tried to catch me, but I ran. And when I ran, all the dogs started to chase me. He had huge arms and he tried to catch me. Oh, Mama! Do I have to go back to the palace?" she sobbed and threw herself on her mother's blanket.

Mama held her trembling young daughter and said, "We are at war, my child. The Berber enemies are at the gates of the city. Your father is in the army. We are alone."

"I know, Mama."

"I can't make enough money to keep you, Cristina. You have to help. You're big enough now. And when you work at the palace, you are fed for free."

"I know... It's not the work ... or the girls who are so cruel to me. It's... It's the *dark*. I hate the dark. Giants get you in the dark."

Mama took her daughter by the hand and pulled her to her feet in the soft darkness of the room. She led her to the door and pulled it open. She looked down the street. "See? No giants."

"On the corner, two streets down from the church," the girl breathed.

"Let's go and look at this giant, shall we?"

"No!" Cristina squeaked.

"Yes, I would like to see him. I was always taught that giants were just monsters from old tales. I would like to meet one."

The woman took her daughter firmly by the hand and led her out into the starlit streets. She pulled the girl up the hill, back towards the palace, past the church.

"Where is the giant?" Mama asked.

Cristina raised a thin finger and pointed towards the groaning, rustling shape ahead of them.

The woman nodded.

"As I thought. It is Master Sancho's windmill. The city needs his flour, so he works all night to feed us."

"No giant arms?" the girl asked.

"Just windmill sails," her mother said. "But if they scare you so much, then on the next feast night, come back across the fields."

"Yes, Mama ... wait for me, Mama!"
Cristina cried and ran home.

But on the next night, the girl
again ran from the palace and
almost fell into the house in her
fearful, fainting state.

"I saw a Berber... He tried to
catch me, but I ran. I almost ran
into him in the dark. I bumped into
him and he smelled terrible. It must
be a Berber... They've broken into
the city."

Mama took her daughter by the hand and pulled her to the door. "Let's take a look at this Berber."

And in the fields, the sour-smelling monster stood, flapping in the wind and grinning at the cloudy sky.

Mama shook her head.

"A scarecrow, Cristina. It's just a scarecrow. You are a *babieca*."

"What's that, Mama?"

"An idiot, Cristina. I'm sorry, but you are an *idiot*."

Chapter Two
Ham
and Horse

Cristina slept badly, with dreams of scarecrows that snatched at her hair and spun her round like the sails of a windmill.

The sun rose into another blue sky and another hot day lay ahead.

Cristina would sweat over the cooking fires in the castle kitchens and taste no cool air till the evening. She plodded wearily up the hill, looking at the dusty road and keeping her bare feet away from sharp stones. Suddenly, there was a monstrous crashing of iron on stone as a troop of knights rode down from the castle.

Every huge warhorse was led by a young man in a tunic of his master's colours. Pictures of swords and dragons, crowns and leopards in reds and golds, blues and silvers, purples and greens and whites.

Their armour glittered, and flags on the tips of their lances made a rainbow of colour.

Cristina was dazzled, and stood gaping while the hooves made sun-bright sparks on the paved street.

An old man dragged her into a doorway. "Don't step in front of that lot, foolish girl!" he said.

"Where are they going?" she asked.

"To attack the Berbers, of course," he laughed. "Those Berbers have been sitting outside our walls for months while we get short of food and water. Now El Cid will lead out his knights and slaughter them all.

There will be blood and Berber
bodies to mop up tonight! Hee!
Hee!"

"Who is El Cid?" Cristina asked.

The old man pointed to the
warrior who rode on the white
horse at the front. "That man there."

Cristina studied the face of the leading knight. "That's Lord Rodrigo," she argued. "I've served him at feasts."

The old man sighed. "Lord Rodrigo Díaz is King Alfonso's greatest warrior ... so the people call him El Cid – The Champion."

"I see. And will he beat the Berbers?" Cristina asked.

"The Berbers know all about him," the old man said. "When I was a soldier, I learned that battles are not won by the best fighters – they are won by the bravest. A scared army is a beaten army."

"And the Berbers are scared of El Cid?"

The man nodded, his eyes glinting in the light of the gleaming armour.

"Oh, yes. Their soldiers will tremble, their swords will shake and their arrows will rattle in their bows. Their teeth will chatter and their legs will be ready to run like rabbits."

"Just by *looking* at El Cid?"
Cristina smiled. "But I served him
roast ham and cabbage last night.
He is such a gentle man."

"He is a lion in battle. And he
is riding a lion, Babieca."

The dust from the hooves filled
the warm air and choked Cristina.
"Don't call me that. My mother
calls me that. It isn't nice."

"Eh?" the man asked, and
scratched his thin, grey beard.
"I didn't call you anything."

"You called me *babieca* – idiot," said Cristina.

"I said that El Cid is *riding* a lion, *Babieca*. His *horse* is called Babieca."

"Is it?" Cristina blinked and rubbed dust from her eyes. The last of the horses had passed. Trumpets sounded and a great cheer rose from the army on the city walls as El Cid and his knights rode out.

The old man hobbled up the hill towards the palace, and Cristina fell into step with him.

"Babieca is El Cid's warhorse," the man explained. "The Champion's godfather was a monk. His gift to young Rodrigo was his pick of any horse from the stable.

"El Cid picked a horse that his godfather thought was weak and useless. The monk cried 'Babieca!'.

Rodrigo laughed and said 'That's a good name for him!' and so the horse is known as Babieca. Of course, it has proved the greatest warhorse in all of Spain."

"Even an idiot can be a hero," Cristina sighed. "I wish I could be a hero ... but I'm such a coward. I'm scared of scarecrows in the dark."

The old man smiled. "We are all heroes. You never know how brave you are until you are tested. Trust me, girl – one day you will find you have a heart as big as Babieca."

Chapter Three
Boar
and Blood

The palace kitchen was busier than ever that day. And it was full of excitement.

Lord Rodrigo's wife, Jimena, came into the kitchens with orders for roast swans and whole boar with apple sauce. Tonight there would be a great party for the knights' victory.

"Have they won, then?" Cristina asked a cook, Ramon.

"Not yet," the red-faced, sweating man spat. "But we will, of course. El Cid is the master of terror. The enemy never know what he will do next. That is why Rodrigo is known as The Champion. The Champion of Terror!"

The palace servants worked all day, and by sunset the tables were piled with the richest food Valencia had. The poor people in the city may be starving, but the knights would eat like gods.

Yet when the doors to the grand hall opened, it was a quiet and miserable troop of dusty knights that wandered in.

"Did we lose?" Cristina asked.

Ramon scowled. "I don't know," he said. "But our lord Rodrigo is not with his knights."

The girl was about to ask more when Lady Jimena burst through the kitchen door and spoke to Ramon in an excited voice. "I want food for my lord Rodrigo."

The cook bowed low and began to say, "The feast is ready in the grand hall, as you ordered—"

But she cut him off. "To my lord's room. Broth. A simple broth with a little bread and warm milk."

"Is he unwell?" Ramon gasped.

Lady Jimena turned on him, furious. "It is not for *you* to ask questions. Just do as you're told."

Ramon shrank and bowed again. "I will bring the broth..."

"No, I don't want you in there. Send this girl," she said, pointing to Cristina.

"As you wish, my lady," the cook cringed.

Jimena was gone and Ramon hurried to obey. He found a small tray for Cristina to carry and led the way to the servants' stairs. "Up here and it's the large double doors ahead of you."

The girl took the tray and made her way up the dim stairway to the top. It led to a corridor and finally

to the doors, which were guarded
by a weary knight.

The knight stopped her, picked
up the spoon and tasted the soup.

"It's not poisoned," Cristina said.
"We would never do that."

The knight opened the door and
let her into the bedroom. Jimena sat
at one side of a great bed that had
curtains pulled back. The shutters

were closed and the room was gloomy. A doctor was standing over a man, who lay on the bed. "Put the food down on this table," the doctor said. "He may eat something later."

Cristina did as she was told and backed towards the door.

"Here, girl, hold this bandage tight while I cut it," snapped the doctor.

Cristina came near the bed and saw Lord Rodrigo lying there. A bandage was wrapped around his throat. As she watched, the cream linen cloth began to turn red with blood.

"Can't you stop the bleeding?" Lady Jimena moaned. "It's only an arrow ... just an unlucky, stray arrow."

"But it has gone deep into the neck – just where his helmet joins with his breastplate," the doctor said.

Lord Rodrigo, El Cid, gave a gurgling moan. Frothy blood trickled from his mouth and he half choked on it while the doctor looked on, helpless. The lord gave one last cry and went still.

The doctor lifted the knight's wrist. He shook his head and looked across the bed at Lady Jimena. "I'm sorry, my lady. Your lord is dead. El Cid is no more."

Lady Jimena looked at the doctor and then at Cristina. "Then we are all dead. All dead," she said.

Chapter Four
Candle
and a Coward

"I'm not dead!" Cristina whispered.

Lady Jimena reached across and stroked the girl's dark hair. "No, my child, no. But today the Berbers saw Lord Rodrigo fall. They chased our knights back into Castile. We only just closed the gates in time."

"But the walls will keep them out!" Cristina argued.

The doctor sighed and spoke slowly. "The Berbers will sit there and stop food getting into the city.

When hunger and disease have made us weak, they will attack and swarm over the walls. They will show no mercy. They may spare the life of a poor girl like you, but they will make you their slave."

Lady Jimena shook her head. "I think they will not wait. The plains are burning with the summer sun. I think they will want to finish us off quickly. I think they will attack tomorrow."

The three sat around the body of their lost leader.

"The Berbers are brave, but Lord Rodrigo terrified them," the doctor sighed. "Just the sight of him made them turn and run."

"I'm the same with windmills ... and I'm even afraid of scarecrows," Cristina said. "The other night I ran home crying because a man of sticks and straw frightened me. I am a coward."

"No, you're not," Lady Jimena said softly. "You didn't run away from a man of sticks and straw! You ran away from a man in the dark. You didn't know he was just a scarecrow."

Cristina nodded. "If I'd known it wasn't a real man, I wouldn't have run," she agreed.

Lady Jimena frowned. "If the Berbers know Lord Rodrigo is dead, they won't run," she said slowly. "But if they thought he was still *alive*..."

"They wouldn't attack tomorrow," the doctor said.

"But he *is* dead," Cristina said. "Dead as a scarecrow."

Lady Jimena turned her wide, brown eyes on the girl. They shone in the light of the single candle by the bed. "But no one *knows*. Only you, and Doctor Alvarez, and me."

"You mean ... we tell everyone that Lord Rodrigo is *alive*?" Cristina asked.

"That won't work!" the doctor moaned. "The Berbers won't believe it ... unless they see him."

"So, let them see him!" Cristina cried, for she suddenly knew what Lady Jimena was thinking. "Show them a scarecrow!"

The doctor almost laughed. "Dress our dead master in his armour? Put rods and straw inside to keep him upright? But how do we march him onto the battlefield?"

"Let him ride!" Cristina said. "Let Babieca carry him into battle."

This time the doctor did laugh. "It would never work. Babieca is a warhorse. He needs someone to ride him ... or lead him. We can't just put a corpse on his back and expect him to lead the troops on to the field of battle."

"Get a squire to lead him," Cristina said. "All the knights have young men to help them!"

"No!" Lady Jimena said sharply. "The city is full of spies. No one, *no one* must know that my husband is dead. We cannot trust a squire, or even a servant – there are even some knights 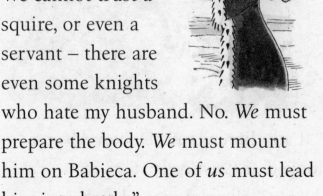 who hate my husband. No. *We* must prepare the body. *We* must mount him on Babieca. One of *us* must lead him into battle."

The doctor shook his head, uncertain. "My lady, my legs are too old to walk through the town and through the gates and onto the fields outside the city."

"And I cannot do it ... everyone knows me. It would look odd. The Berbers would know it was some sort of trick."

Lady Jimena and Doctor Alvarez looked at Cristina.

"Me?" the girl gasped.

Some words echoed in her head. She remembered them from that morning. *We are all heroes. You never know how brave you are until you are tested.*

The time had come for Cristina the coward to be tested.

"I'll do it," she said. "If you will help me, I'll do it."

Chapter Five
Wood
and War

Cristina's first task was to run down to the kitchen to fetch wood and straw. When she reached the kitchen door, she took a deep breath to calm herself.

"What are you doing, girl?" the cook Ramon asked. "You were meant to take broth to El Cid, not take bowls to the Berber army, too. Where have you been?" Before she could answer, he went on, "Not that you are needed. The knights aren't

hungry tonight. They are too
miserable about El Cid's wound."

"He'll live to fight another day,"
said Cristina.

Ramon smiled a wide smile. "Did
you hear that, everyone? Our lord
Rodrigo is alive and well!"

The cheerful servants went into
the great hall to spread the news, and
soon the noise from the hall was as
great as when a battle had been won.

Cristina sweated beside the fire,
looking for firewood that might fit
inside Lord Rodrigo's armour and
keep him straight. Then she slipped
round to the stables to steal hay
from the horses.

Babieca was eating quietly and he turned his white head towards her. Cristina had always been afraid of horses. She reached out a hand and stroked the great charger on the nose. It was softer than any silk she had ever felt. Babieca snorted softly. Cristina managed to smile and let out a long breath. "You like me, then? That will help."

She took the scarecrow stuffing back to the bedroom. The guard gave her a curious look, but Lady Jimena came to the door and told him the girl could come and go freely.

The doctor had cleaned the arrow wound on El Cid's neck and the blood had stopped flowing. Cristina knew that only happened when an animal died. Lady Jimena dressed him in a clean, white shirt and then she helped the doctor strap the knight's armour back in place.

By the time they'd finished, the palace was quiet. The knights had gone off to their beds, to be ready for battle the next day. Lady Jimena told the guard outside the door to get himself some supper in the kitchens.

When the corridors were empty,
the three struggled to carry the
corpse down to the stables. Lady
Jimena was strong, and Cristina
found new strength to help her.

Babieca the warhorse was wary
of the scent of the dead man. As the
doctor and the lady struggled to

push El Cid over the saddle, Cristina
spoke quietly to the horse and
stroked his nose.

They found straps to bind the
warrior's legs to the stirrups, and the
wooden frame under the armour
was tied to the back of the saddle.

Anyone close by could see how El
Cid was held there. But the Berbers
would not be that close.

Lady Jimena climbed onto the side of the stall with El Cid's helmet and slid it into place. Finally, they dressed the girl in a squire's tunic and placed a wide, leather hat on her head to hide her face.

The scarecrow knight was ready, and the cockerel crowed to tell them dawn was breaking.

Lady Jimena was as dusty as the stable floor and hurried off to change while the doctor sank into the straw, exhausted.

Sleepy grooms and squires began to enter the stables. When they saw Cristina holding Babieca, they woke up and began to race to get their own knights' horses ready.

Lady Jimena was soon changed into a fine, silk dress and came back to give orders to the knights. She stood at the head of Babieca and called to the men in armour.

"My lord Rodrigo has hurt his throat with the scratch from that arrow. He has lost his voice. But he has written what he wants you to do."

She read from a sheet of paper: "Ride out and form a line facing our Berber enemies. The foot soldiers will form lines behind you. The Berbers will think El Cid is dead and they will become careless. When you are all lined up and ready, then my lord will ride out and stand on the hilltop behind you."

The knights nodded and began their march through the dust-choked streets of the city. They reached the gates and followed the orders of Lady Jimena. The Berber army had risen with the sun and they were in a happy mood.

Inside the city gates, Lady Jimena whispered to Cristina. "Scared?"

"Yes," Cristina said.

"Not as scared as the Berbers will be when they see El Cid ride out!" the lady said.

Cristina laughed and her fear melted. She led Babieca out on to the hilltop. Babieca, the idiot, led by Cristina ... the *babieca*.

From her place above the battlefield, the coward-girl saw it all. The Berber army seemed to take a step backwards when she appeared. By the time the knights of Castile charged, they were almost running away.

The defeat of the Berbers that day is there in the history books ... and

so is the tale of El Cid's last battle –
the knight of sticks and straw.

The girl turned to the horse. "I'll
never be scared of scarecrows again,"
she said.

You never know how brave you
are until you are tested.

Cristina the *babieca* had passed
the test.

Epilogue

Rodrigo Díaz de Vivar, known as El Cid, was born around the year 1040, so he was almost 60 years old when he died in battle with the Berbers. He lived in Castile in Spain and his country was for ever under attack from armies from North Africa – enemies like the Berbers.

Rodrigo trained as a knight, and was so good the king made him Chief General of the Castile army. In one battle against Aragon, Rodrigo faced a mighty enemy knight. The two men fought hand to hand while their armies looked on. Rodrigo won, and from then on he was known as El Cid – The Champion.

El Cid was a great war leader because he found new ways to defeat the enemies of Castile. He would surprise enemy armies by doing something they didn't expect. He also liked to frighten his enemies – he thought a scared enemy was a beaten enemy, even before the battle started.

In 1074 (aged 34), Rodrigo married Jimena of Oviedo. (She may have been the daughter of El Cid's greatest enemy.) She was said to be one of the most beautiful women in the world.

For about seven years, Rodrigo was sent away from Castile because he upset King Alfonso. He often upset great lords! But when Castile was under attack, the king begged El Cid to come home. Rodrigo became so powerful he was almost a king in his own land.

Then, in 1099, the Berbers attacked Valencia. Rodrigo rode out to attack Berber food and treasure stores, but was hit by an arrow and died.

It is said that Queen Jimena had the idea of tying his corpse to the horse so he could ride out one last time. The Berbers had thought he was dead ... and they were right! When El Cid

appeared, they were so terrified
they ran away, back to their
boats.

The story of his horse –
Babieca the stupid – is supposed
to be true. The horse lived to the
age of 40, but after his master
died no one ever rode him again.
Babieca died two years after
El Cid.

TERRY DEARY'S
GREEK TALES

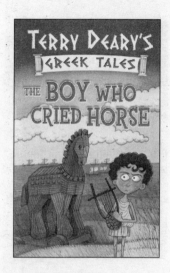

TERRY DEARY'S ROMAN TALES

THE GOOSE GUARDS

THE CAPTIVE CELT

THE FATAL FIRE

THE GRIM GHOST